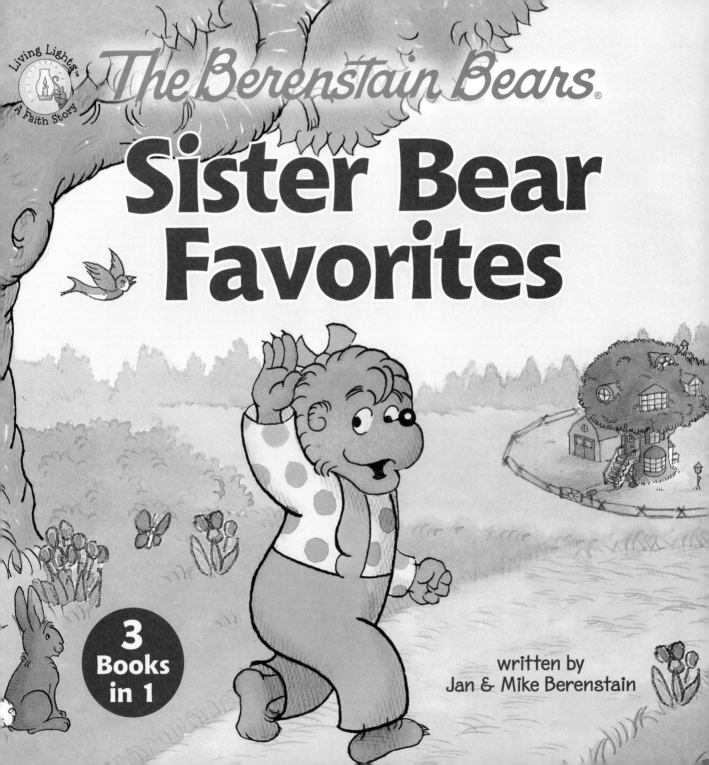

ZONDERKIDZ

The Berenstain Bears Sister Bear Favorites
Copyright © 2019 by Berenstain Publishing, Inc.
Illustrations © 2019 by Berenstain Publishing, Inc.

Requests for information should be addressed to:
Zonderkidz, 3900 Sparks Dr. SE, Grand Rapids, Michigan 49546

Hardcover ISBN 978-0-310-76916-3
Ebook ISBN 978-0-310-76917-0

The Berenstain Bears® and The Golden Rule ISBN 9780310712473 (2008)
The Berenstain Bears'® Gossip Gang ISBN 9780310720850 (2011)
The Berenstain Bears® Why Do Bears Have Bad Days? ISBN 9780310763703 (2019)

Art direction: Diane Mielke

Printed in China

19 20 21 22 23 24 /DSC/ 10 9 8 7 6 5 4 3 2 1

The Berenstain Bears®
Sister Bear Favorites

written by
Jan & Mike Berenstain

Do to others what you would have them do to you.

—Matthew 7:12

The Berenstain Bears and the Golden Rule

Bear Country School

Created by Stan and Jan Berenstain
Written by Mike Berenstain

When Sister Bear received a beautiful golden locket for her birthday, she was surprised and pleased. It was shaped like a heart, and it had her name on it.

"Happy birthday, dear!" said Mama and Papa Bear, giving her a big hug.

Sister tried the locket on and looked at herself in the mirror. "I love it!" she said. "I'm going to wear it all the time."

"It opens up," said Papa. "Look!" He showed her the little golden clasp that you pressed to pop the locket open.

"Neat!" said Sister.

She looked inside, expecting to find a little picture or a mirror or something. But all that she could see inside the locket were a few simple words: "Do to others what you would have them do to you."

Sister was puzzled. The words seemed familiar. But she wasn't sure why. "What's this?" she asked.

"It's the golden rule," explained Mama.

"What's that?" Sister wondered.

Do to others
what you
would have them
do to you

Mama's eyes widened. "The golden rule is one of the most important rules there is," she explained. "That's why we have always had it hanging up on the wall of our living room." She pointed to the framed sampler above their mantelpiece.

Sister gazed up at it in amazement. She had seen that sampler every day of her life. No wonder the words seemed familiar! "Oh," she said, a little embarrassed. "I never really thought about what it said before. What does it mean?"

"The golden rule," Papa explained, "tells you to treat other people the way you want to be treated yourself."

"Why is it inside my locket?" she wondered.

"It's a *golden* rule inside a *golden* locket for a little *golden* princess!" said Papa, giving her a big kiss.

"It's called the golden rule," explained Mama, patiently, "because it's precious, just like gold. But it's not about the gold you wear around your neck or on your finger." She held out her wedding ring. "It's about the golden treasure we keep inside our own hearts. The heart shape of the locket is meant to remind you of that."

Sister thought it over. She didn't really get it. But that was okay. She loved the new locket anyway.

The next day before school, Sister showed off her new
treasure to her friends Lizzy, Millie, Anna, and Linda.
They oohed and ahhed over it in a very satisfying way.
"What's all the fuss about?" asked a voice.

It was Queenie McBear and her gang. Queenie was older than Sister and a little snooty. When Queenie first came to the neighborhood, she and Sister did not get along at all. Queenie made fun of her and got Sister's friends to join in. That was Sister's first experience with an in-crowd—a group that makes itself feel big by making others feel small.

"Oh, hi Queenie," said Sister. "I was just showing the kids my new locket."

Over the years, Sister learned to get along with Queenie. But they never were the best of friends.

"Let's see!" said Queenie.

She looked the locket over. She was not impressed. She herself wore big hoop earrings and lots of beads and chains.

"Cute," was all she said as she walked away with her friends.

Queenie still had her own in-crowd. They were a group of the older girls who liked hanging out together and acting cool. Mostly, they spent their time painting their nails and giggling about boys.

That was okay with Sister. She had her own group of friends to hang out with. But it never occurred to her that this might be any kind of problem until the new girl came to school.

Her name was Suzy MacGrizzie. It seemed like a funny sort of name. For one thing, it had a lot of Zs in it. The new girl herself seemed a little funny too. Her clothes weren't exactly cool, and she wore her hair up in pigtails, which was definitely not the standard Bear Country School style. Besides, she had thick glasses and braces—not the cool kind with lots of different colors like Millie wore—just plain old braces.

On her first day, of course, the new girl didn't know anyone at all. At recess, Sister noticed her standing off by herself in a corner of the playground. She looked sort of sad and lonely. Sister was thinking about going over and introducing herself when Lizzy and Anna came up.

"Hiya, Sister!" said Lizzy. "We're getting together a game of hopscotch. Millie and Linda are over there. Come on!"

Sister began to follow them. But she paused and glanced back to where the new girl was standing all by herself. The new girl looked lonelier than ever.

"Wait a minute," said Sister. "What about that new girl—that what's-her-name—the one over there? Maybe we should invite her to join in. She looks pretty lost and lonely."

The other girls were surprised.

"Suzy Whoozy-face?" said Lizzy, doubtfully.

"She has weird clothes," said Anna.

"And those corny pigtails," said Lizzy.

"Not to mention those clunky glasses and braces," added Anna.

"Well," said Sister, discouraged, "I just thought …"

"Oh, don't worry about old Suzy MacWhoozy!" said Lizzy, taking Sister's arm. "She'll be fine. She'll find some other cubs to play with—cubs more her type. Come on!"

Sister allowed herself to be led away to the hopscotch game. She felt a little worried about Suzy MacWhoozy, though she couldn't exactly say why. But she soon forgot all about it while playing hopscotch with her friends.

Later, when school let out, Sister got in line for her school bus. She noticed that the new girl was standing right in front of her. She was going to say hi, but then Lizzy came up behind her, and they started to talk. They went on talking as they got on the bus.

Suzy MacGrizzie sat right behind them. Sister and Lizzy went right on talking together. Sister played with her new locket as she talked, twirling it around and around in the air.

When the bus came to her stop, Sister gathered up her things to get off. But she felt a soft tug at her arm. It was Suzy MacGrizzie. She was holding something out to Sister.

"Here," she said shyly. "You dropped this." It was Sister's new locket!

"Gee," said Sister. "Thanks!" It was all she could think of to say.

Sister climbed off the bus and watched as it pulled away. She could see Suzy looking back at her from the window. Sister hung her locket back around her neck. What if Suzy hadn't noticed her drop it? It might have been gone for good.

Mama was waiting for Sister as she climbed the front
steps. "How was school today, dear?" asked Mama.

"Oh, okay, I guess," sighed Sister, dumping her
schoolbag on the armchair in the living room. She glanced
up at the framed sampler of the golden rule over the mantel.

Somehow, the golden locket hanging around her neck
felt heavier than before.

That evening at dinner, Sister was unusually thoughtful. She picked at her lima beans and stared off into space.

"A penny for your thoughts," said Papa as he fed Honey Bear.

"Huh?" said Sister, looking up. "Oh, I was just thinking about that golden rule inside my locket," she explained. "I don't really get it. What's it supposed to mean?"

"Well," began Mama. "Let me give you an example. Do you remember that trouble you had when Queenie first moved to town?"

Sister perked up and paid attention. She remembered it all too well.

"Do you remember how Queenie started an in-crowd but kept you out and made fun of your clothes and hair bow?" Mama asked. "Do you remember how badly you felt?"

Boy, did she ever! Sister started to feel hurt just thinking about it. Her lower lip began to quiver, and a tear came to her eye.

"All the golden rule is saying," Papa continued, "is that you shouldn't turn around and do that same sort of thing to someone else."

He paused to scrape some mashed potatoes off Honey's chin. "You should always treat other people the way you would like to be treated yourself."

"But I would never do anything like that!" said Sister. "Besides, I don't have an in-crowd."

"Oh no?" said Brother, who had been taking all this in. "What about Lizzy and Anna and Millie and Linda? You play with them all the time. But I never see you asking anyone else to join in!"

"That's different!" protested Sister, angrily. "I'm just playing with my friends! We're not trying to keep anybody out!"

"Of course not, dear!" soothed Mama. "I'm sure you and your friends would never dream of keeping other cubs out of your group."

Sister Bear grew very quiet. Now that she thought it over, she wasn't quite so sure—not so sure at all!

The next day at recess, as soon as Sister came outside, she looked around the playground for Suzy MacGrizzie. She soon spotted her, sitting off by herself under the big oak tree at the edge of the schoolyard and reading a book.

Sister marched right up to her.
"Hello, Suzy!" she said brightly.

Suzy looked up in surprise.
"Hello," she said shyly.

"I'm Sister Bear, and my
friends and I are going to play
some hopscotch," Sister told her.
"Would you like to join us?"

Suzy's face lit up. "Oh, I'd love
to!" she said with a big bracey grin.
"I love hopscotch!"

"Terrific!" said Sister. "Do you want to see my locket?"

"Sure!" said Suzy.

"Okay," said Sister. "Come on! I'll show it to you ... over there."

Sister took off, and Suzy chased her, laughing, across the playground to the hopscotch square where Lizzy, Millie, Anna, and Linda were waiting.

Sister's golden locket gleamed in the sun as she ran.

"Without wood a fire goes out;
without gossip a quarrel dies down."

—Proverbs 26:20

The Berenstain Bears'
Gossip Gang

written by
Jan & Mike Berenstain

Lizzy and Suzie were Sister Bear's best friends. They liked doing all sorts of things together. They rode bikes and jumped rope.

They played soccer outside and video games inside. They had tea parties with their dolls and stuffed animals. And sometimes they just sat around and talked.

They talked about anything and everything. They talked about TV shows and toys, about games and songs, about pets, parents, brothers and sisters, and, of course, their other friends.

"Did you hear about Queenie?" asked Lizzy. Queenie McBear was an older cub who was very popular. "I heard she has a big crush on Too-Tall Grizzly, but he has a crush on Bonnie Brown!"

"Oooh!" said the others. They were too young to have crushes yet. But they liked to talk about them.

"Did you get a load of that new cub in school?" asked Suzie. "His name is actually Teddy Bear!" The others laughed. Suzie had been a new cub not so long ago. But she didn't seem to remember.

"Well, I saw Anna Bruin the other day," said Sister, "and, you know, I think she put on some weight. She looks sort of chubby."

Lizzy and Suzie giggled.

The three friends talked for a while longer but it was soon dinnertime. "See you!" said Sister, heading home. She liked talking to Lizzy and Suzie about other cubs. It made her feel special and "in-the-know."

Back home, Mama and Papa were setting the table. Brother and Sister joined them.

"Do you know what Herb the mailman told me?" Papa said to Mama as he laid the silverware.

"I can't imagine," said Mama, busy putting out plates.

"He said someone saw Mayor Honeypot throwing a banana peel out his car window. Imagine—the mayor, himself, a litterbug!"

"Now, Papa," said Mama, "you know that's just gossip. You shouldn't spread stories like that."

Papa looked a little ashamed. "I guess you're right. It was just so interesting."

As they sat down to dinner, Sister had a question.

"Mama," she asked, "what's gossip?"

"Well," Mama began, "gossip is when we tell stories about others—especially stories that make them look bad. It's something we do to make ourselves feel special. It can be very hurtful. As the Bible says, 'gossip separates close friends.'"

"Oh," said Sister, worried. She thought maybe saying that Anna looked sort of chubby was gossip. She decided not to think about it anymore.

The next day, Sister saw Lizzy and Suzie walking ahead of her on the way to the playground. They were busy talking and didn't notice Sister coming up behind them. As Sister drew near, she overheard them talking ... about her!

"Do you know what Anna told me about Sister?" began Lizzy.

"No, what?" asked Suzie, eagerly.

"She saw Sister's spelling quiz when Teacher Jane was handing back the papers, and it was marked, '60%—very poor!'" said Lizzy.

"Wow!" said Suzie.

When Sister heard that, she stopped short. In the first place, it wasn't true. Her quiz was marked "70%—fair." That wasn't too good, but it wasn't as bad as all that.

And, in the second place, why were Lizzy and Suzie gossiping about her? They were supposed to be her best friends. She felt so bad she hid behind a tree until Lizzy and Suzie were out of sight.

As Sister came out from behind the tree, Brother Bear walked by. He was on his way to play catch with Cousin Fred.

"What on earth …?" he said. "Why are you hiding behind a tree?"

"I didn't want Lizzy and Suzie to see me," said Sister.

"Why not?" he asked.

"Because they were gossiping about me and I heard," said Sister. "I was so embarrassed!"

"I'm sorry," said Brother. "Why don't you come along with me and play catch with Fred?"
So they did.

At the playground, they started tossing the ball around. Sister could see Lizzy and Suzie on the swings, nearby. They waved and Sister waved back. Then she got angry.

"You know what I heard about Lizzy?' she called, loudly, to Fred.
"I heard that she is a big silly dope!"

"Huh?" said Fred.

"And you know what I heard about Suzie?" she yelled, even louder. "I heard that she is a funny-faced noodle-brain!"

"Sister!" said Brother.

When Lizzy and Suzie overheard Sister, they jumped off the swings and came charging over.

"Why are you saying bad things about us?" they yelled. "We thought you were our best friend!"

"That's just what I thought!" said Sister. "But I heard you gossiping about me on the way here!"

"Oh," said Lizzy. She hadn't thought about it that way. "I guess you're right. We were gossiping about you. I'm sorry!"

"Me too!" said Suzie.

Sister got over being angry right away. After all, Lizzy and Suzie were her best friends.

"That's okay," she said. "Maybe it would be better if we just didn't gossip about anyone."

Lizzy and Suzie agreed. Gossip clearly was more trouble than it was worth.

"As it says in the Bible," said Fred, who liked to memorize
things, "'The tongue also is a fire.'"

"What's that supposed to mean?" said Sister.

"Just that gossiping is like playing with fire," said Fred. "You can
get burnt."

"I think a game of baseball would be a lot more fun than gossip," said Brother.

"Yeah," said Sister. "Let's play!"

"I'll bet me and Fred can beat the three of you, put together," said Brother.

"You're on!" said Sister.
"Play ball!" called Fred.

Sister and her friends won.
After all, it was three against two.

"When I looked for light, then came darkness."
—Job 30:26

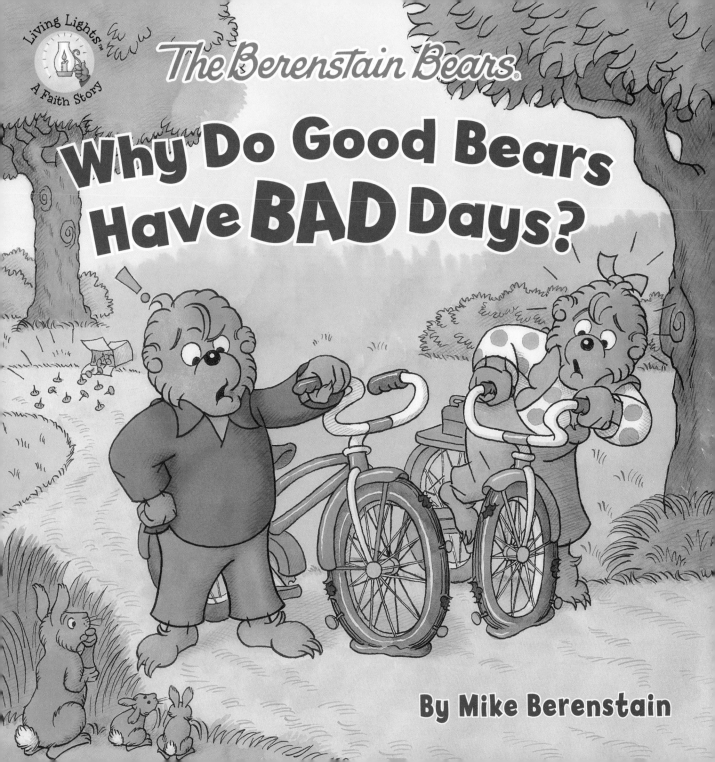

It was the start of a beautiful day, deep in Bear Country. Morning sunlight slanted down as a robin redbreast splashed in a fresh birdbath. At the Bear family's tree house, Brother and Sister came bouncing down the front steps, ready for a day of fishing at the pond. Honey Bear was too young for a long bike ride, so she would stay home to play. The cubs stowed their fishing gear on their bikes and, waving to Mama, Papa, and Honey, eagerly set off.

It was a long ride. Brother and Sister pedaled down the sunny dirt road, past Farmer Ben's farm, around the old honey tree, and through some shadowy woods to a little valley.

There, tucked behind some willows, lay the pond. It was dark and still. Lily pads dotted the surface and dragonflies zipped to and fro. A fish leaped with a *Plop!*

"I'll bet that's the old granddaddy bass I've been wanting to catch," said Brother. "Let's get our lines in the water and see if we can get a bite."

Brother and Sister baited their hooks and cast out. Sister's line went right to the middle of the pond. But Brother's snagged on an overhanging branch.

"Rats," he said, yanking at his line. It was stuck fast. He balanced on a rock to pull it from a different direction.

SPLASH!

But his foot slipped and, with a huge *Splash!* he fell into the pond.

He stood up in the shallows, soaking wet. Sister couldn't help laughing, he looked so funny standing there dripping.

Brother was not amused. Climbing out, he wrung out his shirt and pants. Then he discovered he'd dropped his fishing rod in the pond.

He poked around but couldn't find it.

"Oh, no!" Brother groaned. "No more fishing for me today!"

"Don't worry," Sister said. "I'll share my rod with you."

"Thanks," Brother replied.

"Hey!" Sister hollered. "I think I have a bite."

She began to reel in her line, but her pole bent over more and more.

"Your hook must be caught on something," Brother said.

CRACK!

Sister yanked on her pole, trying to pull the hook loose.

"Careful!" Brother said.

But Sister yanked harder. There was a loud *Crack!* as her fishing rod broke in two.

The cubs stared at the broken rod. With sinking hearts, they realized their day of fishing was over.

"It's not fair!" Sister said as they climbed back on their bikes. "We had the day all planned and, just like that,"—she snapped her fingers—"it's over!"

"Yes," agreed Brother. "Where did we go wrong?"

They slowly pedaled their way out of the valley and through the woods. At least Brother was drying out. But soon they noticed it was getting harder and harder to pedal. Stopping, they found that both bikes had flat tires. Big nails were stuck in each tire.

"What lousy luck!" said Brother. "First, we lose our fishing rods, then this!"

"It's not fair," said Sister again. "We don't deserve it!"

Glumly, the cubs walked their bikes homeward. But it was awkward wheeling the bikes along on flat tires. They made their way around the old honey tree and were passing Farmer Ben's place when they heard a distant rumble.

"Uh, oh!" said Brother. "Thunder!"

They tried to move faster. But dark clouds gathered, and the thunder grew louder. Suddenly, rain swept over them. The cubs were drenched in seconds. The storm quickly passed. But the cubs were thoroughly cold, wet, and miserable.

"This is too much!" said Brother. "First, we lose our fishing rods, then we get flat tires, and now we're soaked!"

"It's not fair," said Sister. "Why is this happening to us?"

That's when they noticed Cousin Fred, Lizzy, and Suzy, coming down the road. They weren't wet—they must have found shelter during the storm.

"Hi, Brother! Hi, Sister!" said Fred. "What happened to you? Did you get caught in the storm?"

"Yes," said Brother. "We've had a really rotten day. First, I fell in the pond and lost my fishing rod. Then, Sister broke her rod in half. Finally, we got flat tires and were drenched by the storm."

"Oh, that's too bad!" said Lizzy. "You know, it makes you wonder why good bears have bad days."

"My grandmother always says it's because God is punishing you for something," said Suzie, matter-of-factly.

"That can't be true!" said Sister. "We haven't done anything wrong. Why would God punish us?"

"Hmm!" said Fred. "You mean you've never done anything wrong in your whole lives?"

"Well," said Sister, "I guess we have ... *sometimes.*"

"Then it's like my grandmother says," said Suzie, shrugging her shoulders. "God must be punishing you for something. See you later."

With a wave, their friends left Brother and Sister to squish their way home.

Back at the tree house, Mama and Papa took charge, whisking Sister and Brother out of their wet clothes and pouring them mugs of hot chocolate. Honey had some too. Brother and Sister felt better but they were still upset about their bad day.

"Mama," said Sister, "why did such bad things happen to us?"

"We met some of our friends on the way home, and they said God must be punishing us for something," added Brother.

Mama and Papa burst out laughing.

"What utter nonsense!" said Mama. "God loves you and watches over you. Even when you make mistakes, he forgives you if you're sorry and try to do better."

"But," asked Brother, "if God is watching over us, why did he let all those bad things happen to us?"

"Son," said Papa, "that's something folks have been asking for a long time. I think the best way to look at it is that God watches over us but he doesn't change the way the world works for our comfort. He's not going to cancel a thunderstorm just because we happen to be outdoors."

"Then, how *does* God watch over us?" wondered Sister.

"I believe God watches over that which he created deep inside us," said Mama. "That special part of us that belongs to him and has faith in him."

"What do you mean?" asked Brother.

"Well," said Papa, "in church, you've heard Preacher Brown talk about our souls, haven't you?"

Brother and Sister nodded.

"Our souls are the part of us that God protects and saves from danger," Papa explained. "No storms or accidents can hurt our souls if we have faith in God."

Brother and Sister thought it over. It was a little hard to understand. But it did make them feel better knowing God was watching over them deep, down inside. And the hot chocolate made them feel better, too, but not as much as the big warm hugs from Mama and Papa.